Ligh[illegible]g [illegible]gs

written by Ann Ketch
illustrated by Joyce Hood

“Look at all the lightning bugs!

“Let’s catch some!”

"I got one!"

"I got one!"

"I got one!"

"I got one!"

"I got another one!"

"Let's show Mom!"

"Hey, Mom, look what we caught!"

"Let's turn off the lights."

“Oh, no! Let’s catc
them… again